THI
AND (

Mildred D. Taylor was born in Jackson, Mississippi, and grew up in Toledo, Ohio. After two years with the Peace Corps she enrolled at the School of Journalism at the University of Colorado where she worked with university officials and fellow students in structuring a Black studies course at the university. She now lives in Colorado.

The Friendship
And Other Stories

MILDRED D. TAYLOR

PUFFIN BOOKS

PUFFIN BOOKS

Published by the Penguin Group
Penguin Books Ltd, 27 Wrights Lane, London W8 5TZ, England
Penguin Books USA Inc., 375 Hudson Street, New York, New York 10014, USA
Penguin Books Australia Ltd, Ringwood, Victoria, Australia
Penguin Books Canada Ltd, 10 Alcorn Avenue, Toronto, Ontario, Canada M4V 3B2
Penguin Books (NZ) Ltd, 182–190 Wairau Road, Auckland 10, New Zealand

Penguin Books Ltd, Registered Offices: Harmondsworth, Middlesex, England

First published in Great Britain by Victor Gollancz Ltd 1989
Published in Puffin Books 1991
3 5 7 9 10 8 6 4

Printed in England by Clays Ltd, St Ives plc

Author's Note

Song of the Trees, *The Friendship* and *The Gold Cadillac* are
all drawn from my family's history and from the stories
told by my family. My family was originally a Mississippi
family. Much of the family had lived in Mississippi since
the days of slavery. Both my maternal and paternal
great-grandparents were born into slavery but with the
Emancipation Proclamation they received their freedom
and in the late 1800's, they bought farm lands of their
own. My grandparents and my parents were born on
those family lands and those lands belong to the family
still.

I was born in Mississippi too, but not on the land. I
was born in the capitol city of Jackson during the days
of World War II. When I was three weeks old, my father
decided to leave Mississippi and the South to go to the
North. Although we had no family in the North, he was

determined that my older sister and I not grow up under the restrictions of segregation that dominated the South. He wanted us to have the freedom and opportunities of the North. A week after he left Mississippi, he got a job at a factory in Toledo, Ohio, and two months later he sent for my mother, my sister, and me; so at three months old, I, still in my mother's arms, took my first ride on a segregated train and left the South.

A year after our arrival in Ohio my parents bought a big house on a busy commercial street. Soon all the many rooms in the big house were needed as the war ended and uncles returned from the fighting overseas, married, and with their brides left the South, and also headed for the freedom and job opportunities of the North. Many other relatives came too, from both my mother's and my father's families. Everyone was looking for freedom and better jobs.

I loved those years we all stayed together in that big house. There were always cousins with whom to play. There was always an aunt or an uncle with whom to talk when my parents were busy, and there seemed always to be fun things to do and plenty of people with whom to do them. On the weekends the whole houseful of family often did things together. Because my father, my uncles and my older male cousins all loved cars, we often rode in a caravan out to the park where the men would park their cars in a long, impressive row and shine them in the shade of the trees while the women spread a picnic and chatted, and my sister, younger cousins and I ran and played. Sometimes we travelled to nearby cities to see other family members or to enjoy a baseball game.

There were times, too, when we took longer trips. My father would prepare the car and my mother would prepare a grand picnic-like dinner and we would head back down two-lane highways into the segregated land of the South. Early, my sister and I learned that though the family had left the South, we had not left the South behind, and each trip down reminded us that the South into which we had been born, the South whose segregated customs and racist laws were rooted in slavery, still remained. As soon as we crossed from the North into the South, the signs reminded us that they remained. On the restrooms of gasoline stations were the signs: WHITE ONLY, COLOURED NOT ALLOWED. Over water fountains were the signs: WHITE ONLY. In restaurant windows, in motel windows, there were always the signs: WHITE ONLY, COLOURED NOT ALLOWED. Every such sign we saw proclaimed our second-class citizenship.

Still, there were two sides of the South I saw. The one of racism, of oppression and segregation, filled me with fear and anger. But the other South, a South of family and community, filled with warmth and love, opened to me a sense of history and filled me with pride. As we sped down winding, red clay roads towards my grandparents' house with rocks hitting the underbelly of the car, my father would begin to point out landmarks of his own childhood or of incidents that had happened. Once we were in my grandparents' house, the house my great-grandfather had built at the turn of the century, the adults would begin to talk about the past and I would begin to visualize all the people who had once lived in that house, all the family who had once known the land, and I felt as if I knew them too. I met them all through the stories told, stories told with such gusto and acting skills that people long since dead lived again through the voices and movements of the storytellers.

I was fascinated by the stories.

Through those stories acted out on moonlit porches or by brightly burning fires, I learned a history about my family going back to the days of slavery. Through those stories I learned a history not then taught in history books, a history about the often tragic lives of black people living in a segregated land. My father told many of the stories. Some of the stories had been told when he was a boy. Some of the stories he actually lived himself. One of the stories my father told was about unwanted lumbermen coming to cut trees on the family land when he was a boy. His vivid descriptions of the giant trees and the events that followed made me feel that I was present too. From this story, I wrote *Song of the Trees*. Another story my father told was about an old black man who refused to call a white man "mister," and in those days in the Southern United States before the Civil Rights Movement, that was a dangerous thing . . . a mighty dangerous thing. From this story, I wrote *The Friendship*. From those years when so many of the family lived in one house in Ohio, I wrote *The Gold Cadillac*. The buying of a brand-new Cadillac was something my father once did. Refusing to ride in the brand-new Cadillac was something my mother once did. The fears of the trip south in a brand-new car were my own.

I hope that readers will enjoy these stories drawn from my life, from my family's history, and from the stories told. The stories as told by my family and the events I lived myself were very special to me and I hope that they will be special, as well, to all who read them.

Contents

Song of the Trees

Song of the Trees

※※※

"Cassie. Cassie, child, wake up now," Big Ma called gently as the new sun peeked over the horizon.

I looked sleepily at my grandmother and closed my eyes again.

"Cassie! Get up, girl!" This time the voice was not so gentle.

I jumped out of the deep feathery bed as Big Ma climbed from the other side. The room was still dark, and I stubbed my toe while stumbling sleepily about looking for my clothes.

"Shoot! Darn ole chair," I fussed, rubbing my injured foot.

"Hush, Cassie, and open them curtains if you can't see," Big Ma said. "Prop that window open, too, and let some of that fresh morning air in here."

I opened the window and looked outside. The earth

was draped in a cloak of grey mist as the sun chased the night away. The cotton stalks, which in another hour would glisten greenly towards the sun, were grey. The ripening corn, wrapped in jackets of emerald and gold, was grey. Even the rich brown Mississippi earth was grey.

Only the trees of the forest were not grey. They stood dark, almost black, across the dusty road, still holding the night. A soft breeze stirred, and their voices whispered down to me in a song of morning greeting.

"Cassie, girl, I said open that window, not stand there gazing out all morning. Now, get moving before I take something to you," Big Ma threatened.

I dashed to my clothes. Before Big Ma had unwoven her long braid of grey hair, my pants and shirt were on and I was hurrying into the kitchen.

A small kerosine lamp was burning in a corner as I entered. Its light reflected on seven-year-old Christopher-John, short, pudgy, and a year younger than me, sitting sleepily upon a side bench drinking a large glass of clabber milk. Mama's back was to me. She was dipping flour from a near-empty canister, while my older brother, Stacey, built a fire in the huge iron-bellied stove.

"I don't know what I'm going to do with you, Christopher-John," Mama scolded. "Getting up in the middle of the night and eating all that cornbread. Didn't you have enough to eat before you went to bed?"

"Yes'm," Christopher-John murmured.

"Lord knows I don't want any of my babies going

hungry, but times are hard, honey. Don't you know folks all around here in Mississippi are struggling? Children crying cause they got no food to eat, and their daddies crying cause they can't get jobs so they can feed their babies? And you getting up in the middle of the night, stuffing yourself with cornbread!''

Her voice softened as she looked at the sleepy little boy. ''Baby, we're in a depression. Why do you think Papa's way down in Louisiana laying tracks on the railroad? So his children can eat—but only when they're hungry. You understand?''

''Yes'm,'' Christopher-John murmured again as his eyes slid blissfully shut.

''Morning, Mama,'' I chimed.

''Morning, baby,'' Mama said. ''You wash up yet?''

''No'm.''

''Then go wash up and call Little Man again. Tell him he's not dressing to meet President Roosevelt this morning. Hurry up now cause I want you to set the table.''

Little Man, a very small six-year-old and a most finicky dresser, was brushing his hair when I entered the room he shared with Stacey and Christopher-John. His blue pants were faded, but except for a small grass stain on one knee, they were clean. Outside of his Sunday pants, these were the only pants he had, and he was always careful to keep them in the best condition possible. But one look at him and I knew that he was far from pleased with their condition this morning. He frowned down at the spot for a moment, then continued brushing.

"Man, hurry up and get dressed," I called. "Mama said you ain't dressing to meet the president."

"See there," he said, pointing at the stain. "You did that."

"I did no such thing. You fell all by yourself."

"You tripped me!"

"Didn't!"

"Did, too!"

"Hey, cut it out, you two!" ordered Stacey, entering the room. "You fought over that stupid stain yesterday. Now get moving, both of you. We gotta go pick blackberries before the sun gets too high. Little Man, you go gather the eggs while Christopher-John and me milk the cows."

Little Man and I decided to settle our dispute later when Stacey wasn't around. With Papa away, eleven-year-old Stacey thought of himself as the man of the house, and Mama had instructed Little Man, Christopher-John, and me to mind him. So, like it or not, we humoured him. Besides, he was bigger than we were.

I ran to the back porch to wash. When I returned to the kitchen, Mama was talking to Big Ma.

"We got about enough flour for two more meals," Mama said, cutting the biscuit dough. "Our salt and sugar are practically down to nothing and—" She stopped when she saw me. "Cassie, baby, go gather the eggs for Mama."

"Little Man's gathering the eggs."

"Then go help him."

20

"But I ain't set the table yet."

"Set it when you come back."

I knew that I was not wanted in the kitchen. I looked suspiciously at my mother and grandmother, then went to the back porch to get a basket.

Big Ma's voice drifted through the open window. "Mary, you oughta write David and tell him somebody done opened his letter and stole that ten dollars he sent," she said.

"No, Mama. David's got enough on his mind. Besides, there's enough garden foods so we won't go hungry."

"But what 'bout your medicine? You're all out of it and the doctor told you good to—"

"Shhhh!" Mama stared at the window. "Cassie, I thought I told you to go gather those eggs!"

"I had to get a basket, Mama!" I hurried off the porch and ran to the barn.

After breakfast, when the sun was streaking red across the sky, my brothers and I ambled into the coolness of the forest leading our three cows and their calves down the narrow cow path to the pond. The morning was already muggy, but the trees closed out the heat as their leaves waved restlessly, high above our heads.

"Good morning, Mr Trees," I shouted. They answered me with a soft, swooshing sound. "Hear 'em, Stacey? Hear 'em singing?"

"Ah, cut that out, Cassie. Them trees ain't singing. How many times I gotta tell you that's just the wind?" He stopped at a sweet alligator gum, pulled out his knife

21

and scraped off a glob of gum that had seeped through its cracked bark. He handed me half.

As I stuffed the gooey wad into my mouth, I patted the tree and whispered. "Thank you, Mr Gum Tree."

Stacey frowned at me, then looked back at Christopher-John and Little Man walking far behind us, munching on their breakfast biscuits.

"Man! Christopher-John! Come on, now," he yelled. "If we finish the berry picking early, we can go wading before we go back."

Christopher-John and Little Man ran to catch up with us. Then, resuming their leisurely pace, they soon fell behind again.

A large grey squirrel scurried across our path and up a walnut tree. I watched until it was settled amidst the tree's feather-like leaves; then, poking one of the calves, I said, "Stacey, is Mama sick?"

"Sick? Why you say that?"

"Cause I heard Big Ma asking her 'bout some medicine she's supposed to have."

Stacey stopped, a worried look on his face. "If she's sick, she ain't bad sick," he decided. "If she was bad sick, she'd been in bed."

We left the cows at the pond and, taking our berry baskets, delved deeper into the forest looking for the wild blackberry bushes.

"I see one!" I shouted.

"Where?" cried Christopher-John, eager for the sweet berries.

22

"Over there! Last one to it's a rotten egg!" I yelled, and off I ran.

Stacey and Little Man followed at my heels. But Christopher-John puffed far behind. "Hey, wait for me," he cried.

"Let's hide from Christopher-John," Stacey suggested.

The three of us ran in different directions. I plunged behind a giant old pine and hugged its warm trunk as I waited for Christopher-John.

Christopher-John puffed to a stop; then, looking all around, called, "Hey, Stacey! Cassie! Hey, Man! Y'all cut that out!"

I giggled and Christopher-John heard me.

"I see you, Cassie!" he shouted, starting towards me as fast as his chubby legs would carry him. "You're it!"

"Not 'til you tag me," I laughed. As I waited for him to get closer, I glanced up into the boughs of my wintry-smelling hiding tree expecting a song of laughter. But the old pine only tapped me gently with one of its long, low branches. I turned from the tree and dashed away.

"You can't, you can't, you can't catch me," I taunted, dodging from one beloved tree to the next. Around shaggy-bark hickories and sharp-needled pines, past blue-grey beeches and sturdy black walnuts I sailed while my laughter resounded through the ancient forest, filling every chink. Overhead, the boughs of the giant trees hovered protectively, but they did not join in my laughter.

Deeper into the forest I plunged.

Christopher-John, unable to keep up, plopped on the ground in a pant. Little Man and Stacey, emerging from their hiding places, ran up to him.

"Ain't you caught her yet?" Little Man demanded, more than a little annoyed.

"He can't catch the champ," I boasted, stopping to rest against a hickory tree. I slid my back down the tree's shaggy trunk and looked up at its long branches, heavy with sweet nuts and slender green leaves, perfectly still. I looked around at the leaves of the other trees. They were still also. I stared at the trees, aware of an eerie silence descending over the forest.

Stacey walked towards me. "What's the matter with you, Cassie?" he asked.

"The trees, Stacey," I said softly, "they ain't singing no more."

"Is that all?" He looked up at the sky. "Come on, y'all. It's getting late. We'd better go pick them berries." He turned and walked on.

"But, Stacey, listen. Little Man, Christopher-John, listen."

The forest echoed an uneasy silence.

"The wind just stopped blowing, that's all," said Stacey. "Now stop fooling around and come on."

I jumped up to follow Stacey, then cried, "Stacey, look!" On a black oak a few yards away was a huge white *X*. "How did that get there?" I exclaimed, running to the tree.

"There's another one!" Little Man screamed.

"I see one too!" shouted Christopher-John.

Stacey said nothing as Christopher-John, Little Man and I ran wildly through the forest counting the ghost-like marks.

"Stacey, they're on practically all of them," I said when he called us back. "Why?"

Stacey studied the trees, then suddenly pushed us down.

"My clothes!" Little Man wailed indignantly.

"Hush, Man, and stay down," Stacey warned. "Somebody's coming."

Two white men emerged. We looked at each other. We knew to be silent.

"You mark them all down here?" one of the men asked.

"Not the younger ones, Mr Andersen."

"We might need them, too," said Mr Andersen, counting the X's. "But don't worry 'bout marking them now, Tom. We'll get them later. Also them trees up past the pond towards the house."

"The old woman agree to you cutting these trees?"

"I ain't been down there yet," Mr Andersen said.

"Mr Andersen . . ." Tom hesitated a moment, looked up at the silent trees, then back at Mr Andersen. "Maybe you should go easy with them," he cautioned. "You know that David can be as mean as an ole jackass when he wanna be."

"He's talking about Papa," I whispered.

"Shhhh!" Stacey hissed.

Mr Andersen looked uneasy. "What's that gotta do with anything?"

"Well, he just don't take much to any dealings with white folks." Again, Tom looked up at the trees. "He ain't afraid like some."

Mr Andersen laughed weakly. "Don't worry 'bout that, Tom. The land belongs to his mama. He don't have no say in it. Besides, I guess I oughta know how to handle David Logan. After all, there are ways . . .

"Now, you get on back to my place and get some boys and start chopping down these trees," Mr Andersen said. "I'll go talk to the old woman." He looked up at the sky. "We can almost get a full day's work in if we hurry."

Mr Andersen turned to walk away, but Tom stopped him. "Mr Andersen, you really gonna chop all the trees?"

"If I need to. These folks ain't got no call for them. I do. I got me a good contract for these trees and I aim to fulfill it."

Tom watched Mr Andersen walk away; then, looking sorrowfully up at the trees, he shook his head and disappeared into the depths of the forest.

"What we gonna do, Stacey?" I asked anxiously. "They can't just cut down our trees, can they?"

"I don't know. Papa's gone . . ." Stacey muttered to himself, trying to decide what we should do next.

"Boy, if Papa was here, them ole white men wouldn't be messing with our trees," Little Man declared.

"Yeah!" Christopher-John agreed. "Just let Papa get

hold of 'em and he gonna turn 'em every which way but loose."

"Christopher-John, Man," Stacey said finally, "go get the cows and take them home."

"But we just brought them down here," Little Man protested.

"And we gotta pick the berries for dinner," said Christopher-John mournfully.

"No time for that now. Hurry up. And stay clear of them white men. Cassie, you come with me."

We ran, brown legs and feet flying high through the still forest.

By the time Stacey and I arrived at the house, Mr Andersen's car was already parked in the dusty drive. Mr Andersen himself was seated comfortably in Papa's rocker on the front porch. Big Ma was seated too, but Mama was standing.

Stacey and I eased quietly to the side of the porch, unnoticed.

"Sixty-five dollars. That's an awful lot of money in these hard times, Aunt Caroline," Mr Andersen was saying to Big Ma.

I could see Mama's thin face harden.

"You know," Mr Andersen said, rocking familiarly in Papa's chair, "that's more than David can send home in two months."

"We do quite well on what David sends home," Mama said coldly.

Mr Andersen stopped rocking. "I suggest you encourage Aunt Caroline to sell them trees, Mary. You know,

27

David might not always be able to work so good. He could possibly have . . . an accident."

Big Ma's soft brown eyes clouded over with fear as she looked first at Mr Andersen, then at Mama. But Mama clenched her fists and said, "In Mississippi, black men do not have accidents."

"Hush, child, hush," Big Ma said hurriedly. "How many trees for the sixty-five dollars, Mr Andersen?"

"Enough 'til I figure I got my sixty-five dollars' worth."

"And how many would that be?" Mama persisted.

Mr Andersen looked haughtily at Mama. "I said I'd be the judge of that, Mary."

"I think not," Mama said.

Mr Andersen stared at Mama. And Mama stared back at him. I knew Mr Andersen didn't like that, but Mama did it anyway. Mr Andersen soon grew uneasy under that piercing gaze, and when his eyes swiftly shifted from Mama to Big Ma, his face was beet-red.

"Caroline," he said, his voice low and menacing, "you're the head of this family and you've got a decision to make. Now, I need them trees and I mean to have them. I've offered you a good price for them and I ain't gonna haggle over it. I know y'all can use the money. Doc Thomas tells me that Mary's not well." He hesitated a moment, then hissed venomously, "And if something should happen to David . . ."

"All right," Big Ma said, her voice trembling. "All right, Mr Andersen."

"No, Big Ma!" I cried, leaping onto the porch. "You can't let him cut our trees!"

28

Mr Andersen grasped the arms of the rocker, his knuckles chalk white. "You certainly ain't taught none of your younguns how to behave, Caroline," he said curtly.

"You children go on to the back," Mama said, shooing us away.

"No, Mama," Stacey said. "He's gonna cut them all down. Me and Cassie heard him say so in the woods."

"I won't let him cut them," I threatened. "I won't let him! The trees are my friends and ain't no mean ole white man gonna touch my trees—"

Mama's hands went roughly around my body as she carried me off to my room.

"Now, hush," she said, her dark eyes flashing wildly. "I've told you how dangerous it is . . ." She broke off in midsentence. She stared at me a moment, then hugged me tightly and went back to the porch.

Stacey joined me a few seconds later, and we sat there in the heat of the quiet room, listening miserably as the first whack of an axe echoed against the trees.

That night I was awakened by soft sounds outside my window. I reached for Big Ma, but she wasn't there. Hurrying to the window, I saw Mama and Big Ma standing in the yard in their night clothes and Stacey, fully dressed, sitting atop Lady, our golden mare. By the time I got outside, Stacey was gone.

"Mama, where's Stacey?" I cried.

"Be quiet, Cassie. You'll wake Christopher-John and Little Man."

"But where's he going?"

"He's going to get Papa," Mama said. "Now be quiet."

"Go on Stacey, boy," I whispered. "Ride for me, too."

As the dust billowed after him, Mama said, "I should've gone myself. He's so young."

Big Ma put her arm around Mama. "Now, Mary, you know you couldn't 've gone. Mr Andersen would miss you if he come by and see you ain't here. You done right, now. Don't worry, that boy'll be just fine."

Three days passed, hot and windless.

Mama forbade any of us to go into the forest, so Christopher-John, Little Man and I spent the slow, restless days hovering as close to the dusty road as we dared, listening to the foreign sounds of steel against the trees and the thunderous roar of those ancient loved ones as they crashed upon the earth. Sometimes Mama would scold us and tell us to come back to the house, but even she could not ignore the continuous pounding of the axes against the trees. Or the sight of the loaded lumber wagons rolling out of the forest. In the middle of washing or ironing or hoeing, she would look up sorrowfully and listen, then turn towards the road, searching for some sign of Papa and Stacey.

On the fourth day, before the sun had risen bringing its cloak of miserable heat, I saw her walking alone towards the woods. I ran after her.

She did not send me back.

"Mama," I said, "how sick are you?"

Mama took my hand. "Remember when you had the flu and felt so sick?"

"Yes'm."

"And when I gave you some medicine, you got well soon afterward?"

"Yes'm."

"Well, that's how sick I am. As soon as I get my medicine, I'll be all well again. And that'll be soon now that Papa's coming home," she said, giving my hand a gentle little squeeze.

The quiet surrounded us as we entered the forest. Mama clicked on the flashlight and we walked silently along the cow path to the pond. There, just beyond the pond, pockets of open space loomed before us.

"Mama!"

"I know, baby, I know."

On the ground lay countless trees. Trees that had once been such strong, tall things. So strong that I could fling my arms partially around one of them and feel safe and secure. So tall and leafy green that their boughs had formed a forest temple.

And old.

So old that Indians had once built fires at their feet and had sung happy songs of happy days. So old, they had hidden fleeing black men in the night and listened to their sad tales of a foreign land.

In the cold of winter when the ground lay frozen, they had sung their frosty ballads of years gone by. Or on a muggy, sweat-drenched day, their leaves had rippled softly, lazily, like restless green fingers strumming at a guitar, echoing their epic tales.

But now they would sing no more. They lay for ever silent upon the ground.

Those trees that remained standing were like defeated warriors mourning their fallen dead. But soon they, too, would fall, for the white X's had been placed on nearly every one.

"Oh, dear, dear trees," I cried as the grey light of the rising sun fell in ghostly shadows over the land. The tears rolled hot down my cheeks. Mama held me close, and when I felt her body tremble, I knew she was crying too.

When our tears eased, we turned sadly towards the house. As we emerged from the forest, we could see two small figures waiting impatiently on the other side of the road. As soon as they spied us, they hurried across to meet us.

"Mama! You and Cassie was in the forest," Little Man accused. "Big Ma told us!"

"How was it?" asked Christopher-John, rubbing the sleep from his eyes. "Was it spooky?"

"Spooky and empty," I said listlessly.

"Mama, me and Christopher-John wanna see too," Little Man declared.

"No, baby," Mama said softly as we crossed the road. "The men'll be down there soon, and I don't want y'all underfoot."

"But, Mama—" Little Man started to protest.

"When Papa comes home and the men are gone, then you can go. But until then, you stay out of there. You hear me, Little Man Logan?"

"Yes'm," Little Man reluctantly replied.

But the sun had been up only an hour when Little

Man decided that he could not wait for Papa to return.

"Mama said we wasn't to go down there," Christopher-John warned.

"Cassie did," Little Man cried.

"But she was with Mama. Wasn't you, Cassie?"

"Well, I'm going too," said Little Man. "Everybody's always going someplace 'cepting me." And off he went.

Christopher-John and I ran after him. Down the narrow cow path and around the pond we chased. But neither of us was fast enough to overtake Little Man before he reached the lumbermen.

"Hey, you kids, get away from here," Mr Andersen shouted when he saw us. "Now, y'all go on back home," he said, stopping in front of Little Man.

"We are home," I said. "You're the one who's on our land."

"Claude," Mr Andersen said to one of the black lumbermen, "take these kids home." Then he pushed Little Man out of his way. Little Man pushed back. Mr Andersen looked down, startled that a little black boy would do such a thing. He shoved Little Man a second time, and Little Man fell into the dirt.

Little Man looked down at his clothing covered with sawdust and dirt, and wailed, "You got my clothes dirty!"

I rushed towards Mr Andersen, my fist in a mighty hammer, shouting, "You ain't got no right to push on Little Man. Why don't you push on somebody your own size—like me, you ole—"

The man called Claude put his hand over my mouth and carried me away. Christopher-John trailed behind us, tugging on the man's shirt.

"Put her down. Hey, mister, put Cassie down."

The man carried me all the way to the pond. "Now," he said, "you and your brothers get on home before y'all get hurt. Go on, get!"

As the man walked away, I looked around. "Where's Little Man?"

Christopher-John looked around too.

"I don't know," he said. "I thought he was behind me."

Back we ran towards the lumbermen.

We found Little Man's clothing first, folded neatly by a tree. Then we saw Little Man, dragging a huge stick, and headed straight for Mr Andersen.

"Little Man, come back here," I called.

But Little Man did not stop.

Mr Andersen stood alone, barking orders, unaware of the oncoming Little Man.

"Little Man! Oh, Little Man, don't!"

It was too late.

Little Man swung the stick as hard as he could against Mr Andersen's leg.

Mr Andersen let out a howl and reached to where he thought Little Man's collar was. But, of course, Little Man had no collar.

"Run, Man!" Christopher-John and I shouted. "Run!"

"Why, you little . . ." Mr Andersen cried, grabbing at Little Man. But Little Man was too quick for him.

He slid right through Mr Andersen's legs. Tom stood nearby, his face crinkling into an amused grin.

"Hey, y'all!" Mr Andersen yelled to the lumbermen. "Claude! Get that kid!"

But sure-footed Little Man dodged the groping hands of the lumbermen as easily as if he were skirting mud puddles. Over tree stumps, around legs and through legs he dashed. But in the end, there were too many lumbermen for him, and he was handed over to Mr Andersen.

For the second time, Christopher-John and I went to Little Man's rescue.

"Put him down!" we ordered, charging the lumbermen.

I was captured much too quickly, though not before I had landed several stinging blows. But Christopher-John, furious at seeing Little Man handled so roughly by Mr Andersen, managed to elude the clutches of the lumbermen until he was fully upon Mr Andersen. Then, with his mightiest thrust, he kicked Mr Andersen solidly in the shins, not once, but twice, before the lumbermen pulled him away.

Mr Andersen was fuming. He slowly took off his wide leather belt. Christopher-John, Little Man and I looked woefully at the belt, then at each other. Little Man and Christopher-John fought to escape, but I closed my eyes and awaited the whining of the heavy belt and its painful bite against my skin.

What was he waiting for? I started to open my eyes, but then the zinging whirl of the belt began and I tensed, awaiting its fearful sting. But just as the leather tip lashed into my leg, a deep familiar voice said, "Put the belt down, Andersen."

I opened my eyes.

"Papa!"

"Let the children go," Papa said. He was standing on a nearby ridge with a strange black box in his hands. Stacey was behind him holding the reins to Lady.

The chopping stopped as all eyes turned to Papa.

"They been right meddlesome," Mr Andersen said. "They need teaching how to act."

"Any teaching, I'll do it. Now, let them go."

Mr Andersen looked down at Little Man struggling to get away. Smiling broadly, he motioned our release. "Okay, David," he said.

As we ran up the ridge to Papa, Mr Andersen said, "It's good to have you home, boy."

Papa said nothing until we were safely behind him. "Take them home, Stacey."

"But, Papa—"

"Do like I say, son."

Stacey herded us away from the men. When we were far enough away so Papa couldn't see us, Stacey stopped and handed me Lady's reins.

"Y'all go on home now," he said. "I gotta go help Papa."

"Papa don't need no help," I said. "He told you to come with us."

"But you don't know what he's gonna do."

"What?" I asked.

"He's gonna blow up the forest if they don't get out of here. So go on home where y'all be safe."

"How's he gonna do that?" asked Little Man.

"We been setting sticks of dynamite since the middle of the night. We ain't even been up to the house cause Papa wanted the sticks planted and covered over before the men came. Now, Cassie, take them on back to the house. Do like I tell you for once, will ya?" Then, without waiting for another word, he was gone.

"I wanna see," Little Man announced.

"I don't," protested Christopher-John.

"Come on," I said.

We tied the mare to a tree, then belly-crawled back to where we could see Papa and joined Stacey in the brush.

"Cassie, I told you . . ."

"What's Papa doing?"

The black box was now set upon a sawed-off tree stump, and Papa's hands were tightly grasping a T-shaped instrument which went into it.

"What's that thing?" asked Little Man.

"It's a plunger," Stacey whispered. "If Papa presses down on it, the whole forest will go pfffff!"

Our mouths went dry and our eyes went wide. Mr Andersen's eyes were wide, too.

"You're bluffing, David," he said. "You ain't gonna push that plunger."

"One thing you can't seem to understand, Andersen," Papa said, "is that a black man's always gotta be ready to die. And it don't make me any difference if I die today or tomorrow. Just as long as I die right."

Mr Andersen laughed uneasily. The lumbermen moved nervously away.

"I mean what I say," Papa said. "Ask anyone. I always mean what I say."

"He sure do, Mr Andersen," Claude said, eyeing the black box. "He always do."

"Shut up!" Mr Andersen snapped. "And the rest of y'all stay put." Then turning back to Papa, he smiled cunningly. "I'm sure you and me can work something out, David."

"Ain't nothing to be worked out," said Papa.

"Now, look here, David, your mama and me, we got us a contract . . ."

"There ain't no more contract," Papa replied coldly. "Now, either you get out or I blow it up. That's it."

"He means it, Mr Andersen," another frightened lumberman ventured. "He's crazy and he sure 'nough means it."

"You know what could happen to you, boy?" Mr Andersen exploded, his face beet-red again. "Threatening a white man like this?"

Papa said nothing. He just stood there, his hands firmly on the plunger, staring down at Mr Andersen.

Mr Andersen could not bear the stare. He turned away, cursing Papa. "You're a fool, David. A crazy fool." Then he looked around at the lumbermen. They shifted their eyes and would not look at him.

"Maybe we better leave, Mr Andersen," Tom said quietly.

Mr Andersen glanced at Tom, then turned back to

Papa and said as lightly as he could, "All right, David, all right. It's your land. We'll just take the logs we got cut and get out." He motioned to the men. "Hey, let's get moving and get these logs out of here before this crazy fool gets us all killed."

"No," Papa said.

Mr Andersen stopped, knowing that he could not have heard correctly. "What you say?"

"You ain't taking one more stick out of this forest."

"Now, look here—"

"You heard me."

"But you can't sell all these logs, David," Mr Andersen exclaimed incredulously.

Papa said nothing. Just cast that piercing look on Mr Andersen.

"Look, I'm a fair man. I tell you what I'll do. I'll give you another thirty-five dollars. An even hundred dollars. Now, that's fair, ain't it?"

"I'll see them rot first."

"But—"

"That's my last word," Papa said, tightening his grip on the plunger.

Mr Andersen swallowed hard. "You won't always have that black box, David," he warned. "You know that, don't you?"

"That may be. But it won't matter none. Cause I'll always have my self-respect."

Mr Andersen opened his mouth to speak, but no sound came. Tom and the lumbermen were quietly moving away, putting their gear in the empty lumber wagons. Mr Andersen looked again at the black box. Finally, his face ashen, he too walked away.

Papa stood unmoving until the wagons and the men were gone. Then, when the sound of the last wagon rolling over the dry leaves could no longer be heard and a hollow silence filled the air, he slowly removed his hands from the plunger and looked up at the remaining trees standing like lonely sentries in the morning.

"Dear, dear old trees," I heard him call softly, "will you ever sing again?"

I waited. But the trees gave no answer.

The Friendship

In memory of my father, the storyteller

The Friendship

"Now don't y'all go touchin' nothin'," Stacey warned as we stepped onto the porch of the Wallace store. Christopher-John, Little Man, and I readily agreed to that. After all, we weren't even supposed to be up here. "And Cassie," he added, "don't you say nothin'."

"Now, boy, what I'm gonna say?" I cried, indignant that he should single me out.

"Just mind my words, hear? Now come on." Stacey started for the door, then stepped back as Jeremy Simms, a blond sad-eyed boy, came out. Looking out from under the big straw hat he was wearing, he glanced somewhat shyly at us, then gave a nod. We took a moment and nodded back. At first I thought Jeremy was going to say something. He looked as if he wanted to, but then he walked on past and went slowly down the steps. We all watched him. He got as far as the corner of the porch and looked back. The boys and I turned and went into the store.

Once inside we stood in the entrance a moment, somewhat hesitant now about being here. At the back counter, two of the storekeepers, Thurston and Dewberry Wallace, were stocking shelves. They glanced over, then paid us no further attention. I didn't much like them. Mama and Papa didn't much like them either. They didn't much like any of the Wallaces and that included Dewberry and Thurston's brother, Kaleb, and their father, John. They said the Wallaces didn't treat our folks right and it was best to stay clear of them. Because of that they didn't come up to this store to shop and we weren't supposed to be coming up here either.

We all knew that. But today as we had walked the red road towards home, Aunt Callie Jackson, who wasn't really our aunt but whom everybody called that because she was so old, had hollered to us from her front porch and said she had the headache bad. She said her nephew Joe was gone off somewhere and she had nobody to send to the store for head medicine. We couldn't say no to her, not to Aunt Callie. So despite Mama's and Papa's warnings about this Wallace place, we had taken it upon ourselves to come anyway. Stacey had said they would understand and after a moment's thought had added that if they didn't he would take the blame and that had settled it. After all, he was twelve with three years on me, so I made no objection about the thing. Christopher-John and Little Man, younger still, nodded agreement and that was that.

"Now mind what I said," Stacey warned us again, then headed for the back counter and the Wallaces. Christopher-John, Little Man, and I remained by the front door looking the store over; it was our first time in the place. The store was small, not nearly as large as it had looked from the outside peeping in. Farm supplies and household and food goods were sparsely displayed on the shelves and counters and the floor space too, while on the walls were plastered posters of a man called Roosevelt. In the centre of the store was a pot-bellied stove, and near it a table and some chairs. But nobody was sitting there. In fact, there were no other customers in the store.

Our eyes roamed over it all with little interest; then we spotted the three large jars of candy on one of the counters. One was filled with lemon drops, another with liquorice, and a third with candy canes. Christopher-John, who was seven, round, and had himself a mighty sweet tooth, glanced around at Little Man and me, grinning. Then he walked over to the candy jars for a closer look. There he stood staring at them with a hungry longing even though he knew good and well there would be no candy for him this day. There never was for any of us except at Christmas-time. Little Man started to follow him, but then something else caught his eye. Something gleaming and shining. Belt buckles and lockets, cuff-links, and tie-clips in a glass case. As soon as Little Man saw them, he forgot about the jars of candy and strutted right over. Little Man loved shiny new things.

47

Not interested in drooling over candy I knew I couldn't have, or shiny new things either, I went on to the back and stood with Stacey. Since the Wallaces were taking their own good time about serving us, I busied myself studying a brand-new 1933 catalogue that lay open on the counter. Finally, Dewberry asked what we wanted. Stacey was about to tell him, but before he could, Dewberry's eyes suddenly widened and he slapped the rag he was holding against the counter and hollered, "Get them filthy hands off-a-there!"

Stacey and I turned to see who he was yelling at. So did Christopher-John. Then we saw Little Man. Excited by the lure of all those shiny new things, Little Man had forgotten Stacey's warning. Standing on tiptoe, he was bracing himself with both hands against the top of the glass counter for a better look inside. Now he glanced around. He found Dewberry's eyes on him and snatched his hands away. He hid them behind his back.

Dewberry, a full-grown man, stared down at Little Man. Little Man, only six, looked up. "Now I'm gonna hafta clean that glass again," snapped Dewberry, "seeing you done put them dirty hands-a yours all over it!"

"My hands ain't dirty," Little Man calmly informed him. He seemed happy that he could set Dewberry's mind to rest if that was all that was bothering him. Little Man pulled his hands from behind his back and inspected them. He turned his hands inward. He turned them outward. Then he held them up for Dewberry to see. "They clean!" he said. "They ain't dirty! They clean!"

Dewberry came from around the corner. "Boy, you disputin' my word? Just look at ya! Skin's black as dirt. Could put seeds on ya and have 'em growin' in no time!"

Thurston Wallace laughed and tossed his brother an axe from one of the shelves. "Best chop them hands off, Dew, they that filthy!"

Little Man's eyes widened at the sight of the axe. He slapped his hands behind himself again and backed away. Stacey hurried over and put an arm around him. Keeping eyes on the Wallaces, he brought Little Man back to stand with us. Thurston and Dewberry laughed.

We got Aunt Callie's head medicine and hurried out. As we reached the steps we ran into Mr Tom Bee carrying a fishing pole and two strings of fish. Mr Tom Bee was an elderly, toothless man who had a bit of sharecropping land over on the Granger Plantation. But Mr Tom Bee didn't do much farming these days. Instead he spent most of his days fishing. Mr Tom Bee loved to fish. "Well now," he said, coming up the steps, "where y'all younguns headed to?"

Stacey nodded towards the crossroads. "Over to Aunt Callie's, then on home."

"Y'all hold on up a minute, I walk with ya. Got a mess-a fish for Aunt Callie. Jus' wants to drop off this here other string and get me some more-a my sardines. I loves fishin' cat, but I keeps me a taste for sardines!" he laughed.

Stacey watched him go into the store, then looked back to the road. There wasn't much to see. There was a lone gas pump in front of the store. There were two red roads that crossed each other, and a dark forest that loomed on the other three corners of the crossroads. That was all, yet Stacey was staring out intensely as if there were more to see. A troubled look was on his face and anger was in his eyes.

"You figure we best head on home?" I asked.

"Reckon we can wait, Mr Tom Bee don't take too long," he said, then leaned moodily back against the post. I knew his moods and I knew this one had nothing to do with Mr Tom Bee. So I let him be and sat down on the steps in the shade of the porch trying to escape some of the heat. It was miserably hot. But then it most days was in a Mississippi summer. Christopher-John sat down too, but not Little Man. He remained by the open doors staring into the store. Christopher-John noticed him there and immediately hopped back up again. Always sympathising with other folks' feelings, he went over to Little Man and tried to comfort him. "Don'tcha worry now, Man," he said, patting his shoulder. "Don'tcha worry! We knows you ain't dirty!"

"That ain't what they said!" shrieked Little Man, his voice revealing the hurt he felt. Little Man took great pride in being clean.

Stacey turned to them. "Man, forget about what they said. You can't pay them no mind."

"But, St-Stacey! They said they could plant seeds on me!" he cried indignantly.

I looked back at him. "Ah, shoot, boy! You know they can't do no such-a thing!"

Sceptically Little Man looked to Stacey for affirmation.

Stacey nodded. "They can do plenty all right, but they can't do nothin' like that."

"But—but, Stacey, th-they s-said they was g-gonna c-cut off my hands. They done s-said they gonna do that c-cause they . . . they dirty!"

Stacey said nothing for a moment, then pulled from the post and went over to him. "They was jus' teasin' you, Man," he said softly, "that's all. They was jus' teasin'. Their way of funnin'."

"Wasn't nothin' 'bout it funny to me," I remarked, feeling Little Man's hurt.

Stacey's eyes met mine and I knew he was feeling the same. He brought Little Man back to the steps and the two of them sat down. Little Man, seemingly comforted with Stacey beside him, was silent now. But after a few moments he did a strange thing. He reached down and placed his hand flat to the dirt. He looked at his hand, looked at the dirt, then drew back again. Without a word, he folded his hands tightly together and held them very still in his lap.

I looked at the ground, then at him. "Now what was all that about?"

Little Man looked at me, his eyes deeply troubled. And once again, Stacey said, "Forget it, Man, forget it."

Little Man said nothing, but I could tell he wasn't forgetting anything. I stared down at the dirt. I wasn't forgetting either.

"'Ey, y'all."

We turned. Jeremy Simms was standing at the corner of the porch.

"Boy, I thought you was gone!" I said.

Stacey nudged me to be quiet, but didn't say anything to Jeremy himself. Jeremy bit at his lip, his face reddening. Rubbing one bare foot against the other, he pushed his hands deep into his overall pockets. "C-come up here to wait on my pa and R.W. and Melvin," he explained. "Got a load to pick up. Been waiting a good while now."

Stacey nodded. There wasn't anything to say to that. Jeremy seemed to understand there was nothing to say. A fly buzzed near his face. He brushed it away, looked out at the crossroads, then sat down at the end of the porch and leaned against a post facing us. He pulled one leg up towards his chest and left the other leg dangling over the side of the porch. He glanced at us, looked out at the crossroads, then back at us again. "Y'all . . . y'all been doin' a lotta fishin' here lately?"

Stacey glanced over. "Fish when we can."

"Over on the Rosa Lee?"

Stacey nodded his answer.

"I fish over there sometimes . . ."

"Most folks do . . ." said Stacey.

Jeremy was silent a moment as if thinking on what he should say next. "Y'all . . . y'all spect to be goin' fishin' again anyways soon?"

Stacey shook his head. "Cotton time's here. Got too much work to do now for much fishin'."

"Yeah, me too I reckon . . ."

52

Jeremy looked away once more and was quiet once more. I watched him, trying to figure him out. The boy was a mighty puzzlement to me, the way he was always talking friendly to us. I didn't understand it. He was white.

Stacey saw me staring and shook his head, letting me know I shouldn't be doing it. So I stopped. After that we all just sat there in the muggy midday heat listening to the sounds of bees and flies and cawing blackbirds and kept our silence. Then we heard voices rising inside the store and turned to look. Mr Tom Bee, the string of fish and the fishing pole still in his hand, was standing before the counter listening to Dewberry.

"Now look here, old uncle," said Dewberry, "I told you three times my daddy's busy! You tell me what you want or get on outa here. I ain't got all day to fool with you."

Mr Tom Bee was a slightly built man, and that along with his age made him look somewhat frail, and especially so as he faced the much younger Dewberry. But that look of frailty didn't keep him from speaking his mind. There was a sharp-edged stubbornness to Mr Tom Bee. His eyes ran over both Dewberry and Thurston and he snapped: "Give me some-a them sardines! Needs me four cans!"

Dewberry leaned across the counter. "You already got plenty-a charges, Tom. You don't need no sardines. Ya stinkin' of fish as it is."

I nudged Stacey. "Now how he know what Mr Tom Bee need?"

Stacey told me to hush.

"Well, shoot! Mr Tom Bee been grown more years than 'bout anybody 'round here! He oughta know what he need!"

"Cassie, I said hush!" Stacey glanced back towards the store as if afraid somebody inside might have heard. Then he glanced over at Jeremy, who bit his lower lip and looked away again as if he had heard nothing at all.

Saying nothing else, Stacey looked back at the crossroads. I cut my eyes at him, then sighed. I was tired of always having to watch my mouth whenever white folks were around. Wishing Mr Tom Bee would get his stuff and come on, I got up and crossed the porch to the doorway. It was then I saw that Christopher-John had eased back inside and was again staring up at the candy jars. I started to tell Stacey that Christopher-John was in the store, then realized Mr Tom Bee had noticed him too. Seeing Christopher-John standing there, Mr Tom Bee pointed to the candy and said to Dewberry, "An' you can jus' give me some-a them candy canes there too."

"Don't need no candy canes neither, Tom," decided Dewberry. "Got no teeth to chew 'em with."

Mr Tom Bee stood his ground. "Y'all can't get them sardines and that candy for me, y'all go get y'alls daddy and let him get it! Where John anyway?" he demanded. "He give me what I ask for, you sorry boys won't!"

Suddenly the store went quiet. I could feel something was wrong. Stacey got up. I looked at him. We both knew this name business was a touchy thing. I didn't really understand why, but it was. White folks took it seriously. Mighty seriously. They took it seriously to call every grown black person straight out by their first name without placing a "mister" or a "missus" or a "miss" anywhere. White folks, young and old, called Mama and Papa straight out by their first names. They called Big Ma by her first name or they sometimes called her aunty because she was in her sixties now and that was their way of showing her age some respect, though Big Ma said she didn't need that kind of respect. She wasn't *their* aunty. They took seriously too the way we addressed them. All the white grown folks I knew expected to be addressed proper with that "mister" and "missus" sounding loud ahead of their names. No, I didn't understand it. But I understood enough to know Mr Tom Bee could be in trouble standing up in this store calling Dewberry and Thurston's father John straight out.

Jeremy glanced from the store to us, watching, his lips pressed tight. I could tell he understood the seriousness of names too. Stacey moved towards me. It was then he saw Christopher-John inside the store. He bit his lip nervously, as if trying to decide if he should bring attention to Christopher-John by going in to get him. I think the quiet made him wait.

Dewberry pointed a warning finger at Mr Tom Bee. "Old nigger," he said, "don't you never in this life speak to me that way again. And don't you never stand up there with yo' black face and speak of my daddy or any other white man without the proper respect. You might be of a forgetful mind at yo' age, but you forgettin' the wrong thing when you forgettin' who you are. A nigger, nothin' but a nigger. You may be old, Tom, but you ain't too old to teach and you ain't too old to whip!"

My breath caught and I shivered. It was such a little thing, I figured, this thing about a name. I just couldn't understand it. I just couldn't understand it at all.

The back door to the store slammed and a man appeared in the doorway. He was average-built and looked to be somewhere in his fifties. The man was John Wallace, Dewberry and Thurston's father. He looked at Mr Tom Bee, then motioned to his sons. "I take care-a this," he said.

Mr Tom Bee grinned. "Well, howdy there, John!" he exclaimed. "Glad ya finally done brought yourself on in here! These here boys-a yours ain't been none too friendly."

John Wallace looked solemnly at Mr Tom Bee. "What ya want, Tom?"

"Wants me my sardines and some candy there, John."

Dewberry slammed his fist hard upon the counter. "Daddy! How come you to let this old nigger disrespect ya this here way? Just lettin' him stand there and talk to you like he was a white man! He need teachin', Daddy! He need teachin'!"

"Dew's right," said Thurston. "Them old britches done stretched way too big!"

John Wallace wheeled around and fixed hard, unrelenting eyes on his sons. "Y'all hush up and get on to ya business! There's stackin' to be done out back!"

"But, Daddy—"

"I said get!"

For a moment Dewberry and Thurston didn't move. The heat seemed more stifling. The quiet more quiet. John Wallace kept eyes on his sons. Dewberry and Thurston left the store.

As the back door closed behind them Stacey went in and got Christopher-John. Mr John Wallace took note of him, took note of all of us, and as Stacey and Christopher-John came out he came behind and closed the doors. But he forgot the open windows. He turned back to Mr Tom Bee. "Now, Tom," he said, "I done told you before 'bout calling me by my Christian name, it ain't jus' the two of us. It ain't seemly, you here a nigger and me a white man. Now you ain't used to do it. Some folks say it's yo' old age. Say your age is making you forget 'bout way things is. But I say it ain't your age, it's your orneriness."

Mr Tom Bee squared his shoulders. "An' I done tole you, it ain't seemly t' me to be callin' no white man mister when I done saved his sorry hide when he wasn't hardly no older'n them younguns standin' out yonder! You owes me, John. Ya knows ya owes me too."

John Wallace walked back to the counter. "Ain't necessarily what I'm wanting, but what's gotta be. You just can't keep going 'round callin' me by my first name no more. Folks been taking note. Makes me look bad. Even my boys been questionin' me on why I lets ya do it."

"Then tell 'em, doggonit!"

"I'm losin' face, Tom."

"Now, what you think I care 'bout your face, boy? I done saved your hide more'n one time and I gots me a right t' call you whatsoever I pleases t' call you whensoever I be talkin' t' ya!"

John Wallace sucked in his breath. "Naw, Tom, not no more."

Mr Tom Bee sucked in his breath too. "You figure the years done made you forget how come you alive an' still breathin'?"

"Figure the years done give me sense 'bout this thing."

"Well, you live long 'nough, maybe the next years gonna give you the sense 'nough t' be grateful. Now put these here sardines on my charges." He glanced over at the candy jars. "An' give me two pennies' worth-a them there candy sticks while's you at it."

Mr Tom Bee stood quietly waiting as if expecting his order to be obeyed, and to our surprise Mr John Wallace did obey. He reached into the candy jar, pulled out a fistful of candy canes, and handed them to him. Mr Tom Bee took the candy canes and gave John Wallace a nod. Mr John Wallace put both hands flat on the counter.

"Tom, mind what I say now. My patience done worn thin 'bout 'mindin' you 'bout what's proper. Next time you come in here, you make sure you address me right, you hear?"

Mr Tom Bee cackled a laugh and slapped one string of fish on the counter. "These here for you, John. Knows how much you like catfish so these here for you!" Then, still chuckling, he picked up his cans of sardines and stuffed them into his pockets, turned his back on John Wallace, and left the store.

As soon as Mr Tom Bee was outside, he looked down at Christopher-John and said, "How'd y'all younguns like a little bit-a candy?"

"Like it just fine, Mr Tom Bee!" spoke up Christopher-John.

Mr Tom Bee laughed and handed him a stick, then presented one each to Stacey, Little Man, and me. Stacey, Christopher-John, and I were mighty thankful, but Little Man only looked joylessly at his candy cane and stuck it into his shirt pocket.

"What's this?" asked Mr Tom Bee. "What's this? Ain't ya gonna eat that candy cane, boy?"

Little Man shook his head.

"Well, why not? Mighty good!"

"Don't want they ole candy canes! They said I was dirty! I ain't dirty, Mr Tom Bee!"

Mr Tom Bee put his hands on his hips and laughed. "Lord have mercy! Course ya ain't, boy! Don't you know them Wallace boys ain't got no more good sense'n a wall-eyed mule! Last thing in the world ya wantin' to be doin' is listenin' to anything they gotta say! They say somethin's red, ya best be figurin' it's green. They say somethin' dirty, ya gotta know it's clean! Shuckies, Little Man! You got more sense with them six years a your'n than them two boys ever gonna see. Don't ya never pay them no mind!"

Little Man thought on that, looked around at Stacey, who nodded his agreement with Mr Tom Bee, then took the candy cane from his pocket and gave it a listless lick.

Then Mr Tom Bee noticed Jeremy and snapped, "You the kinda boy keep hold to yo' promises?"

Jeremy, who seemed taken aback by the question, nodded mutely.

At that, Mr Tom Bee pulled forth another candy cane and held it out to him. The boys and I waited, wondering if Jeremy would take it. Jeremy seemed to be wondering if he should. He hesitated, looked around as if fearful someone other than we would see, and took it. He didn't actually say thank you to Mr Tom Bee, but then the nod he gave and his eyes did. I had a feeling Jeremy didn't see much penny candy either.

As Mr Tom Bee, the boys, and I started down the road, Jeremy called after us. "Stacey! May—maybe one-a these here days, maybe I go fishin' with y'all . . ."

"Yeah . . ." Stacey replied. "Yeah, one-a these days, maybe so . . ."

We headed on towards Aunt Callie's. Stacey sucked thoughtfully at his candy stick, then looked up at Mr Tom Bee. "Mr Tom Bee, something I been thinkin' on."

"What's that, boy?"

"'Bout how come you to call Mr Wallace plain-out by his first name. I mean you don't call him mister or nothin'." He paused. "Don't know nobody else to do, nobody coloured I mean. Fact to business, don't know nobody coloured call a white man straight to his face by his first name."

Mr Tom Bee laughed. "He call me straight-out Tom 'thout no mister, don't he now?"

Stacey nodded. "Yes, sir, that's a fact, but that's the way white folks do. Papa say white folks set an awful store 'bout names and such. He say they get awful riled 'bout them names too. Say they can do some terrible things when they get riled. Say anybody call a white man straight out by his name just lookin' for trouble."

"Well, that's sho the truth all right," agreed Mr Tom Bee. "But shuckies! I ain't studyin' they foolish way-a things and I ain't gonna be callin' that John Wallace no mister neither! He done promised me long time ago I could call him straight out by his name long's I lived an' I aims to see he holds to his promises." He paused, then added, "'Sides, we used t' be friends."

"Friends?" said Stacey as if he didn't understand the word.

"That's right. Me and that John Wallace, we goes way back. Long ways back. Why, shuckies! I done saved that boy's life!"

We all looked up from our candy canes.

"That's right!" he said with an emphatic nod. "Sho did! That John Wallace wasn't no more'n fifteen when I come along the road one day and found him sinkin' in swampland and pulled him out. Asked him what his name was. He said, call me John. So's that what I called him, jus' that. John. But that there was only the first time I done saved his life.

"No sooner'n I done him outa that swampland, I come t' find out he was burnin' up with fever, so's I doctored him. Ain't never laid eyes on the boy before, but I doctored him anyways. Doctored him till I got him well.

Turned out the boy ain't had no family round here. Said he was coming up from down Biloxi way when he landed hisself in that swamp. Anyways, I let him stay on with me till he got hisself strong. Let him stay on long's he wanted and that was for quite some while, till the white folks round started meddlin' 'bout a white boy stayin' wit' me. I done took care-a John Wallace like a daddy woulda and long's he stayed with me, he minded what I said and was right respectful."

Stacey shook his head as if finding that hard to believe.

Mr Tom Bee saw the disbelief and assured him it was so. "That's right! Right respectful, and all that time, I been callin' him John. Jus' that. John. Well, come the day John Wallace tole me he was goin' up to Vicksburg to look for a job an' I said to him I figured next time I see him, I 'spected I'd most likely hafta be callin' him *Mister* John. And he told me things wasn't never gonna be that way. He says to me, I'm John t' you now, gonna always be John t' ya, cause you been like a daddy t' me an' I couldn't never 'spect my daddy to go callin' me mister. He done promised me that. Promised me he wasn't never gonna forget what I done for him. Said he was gonna always owe me. But then he come back down in here some years later to set up that store and things had done changed. He 'spected all the coloured folks to call him 'Mister' John, and that there done included ole Tom Bee."

"Owww," I said, "Mr John Wallace done broke his word!"

"He sho done that all right! Now I been thinkin' here

lately maybe it's time I makes him keep his word. I figures I'm close 'nough to meetin' my Maker, it don't much matter he like it or not. I ain't studyin' that boy!"

I took a lick of candy. "Well, Big Ma—she say you gonna get yourself in a whole lotta trouble, Mr Tom Bee. She say all them years on you done made you go foolish—"

"Cassie!" Stacey rebuked me with a hard look.

I gave him a look right back. "Well, she did!" Not only had Big Ma said it, but plenty of other folks had too. They said Mr Tom Bee had just all of a sudden up and started calling Mr Wallace John. He had started after years of addressing John Wallace like the white folks expected him to do. Most folks figured the only reason for him to do a fool thing like that was because he had gone forgetful, that his advancing years were making him think it was a long time back when John Wallace was still a boy. I told it all. "Said you just full of foolishness callin' that man by his name that way!"

Mr Tom Bee stopped right in the middle of the road, slapped his thighs, and let go a rip of a laugh. "Well, ya know somethin', Cassie? Maybe yo' grandmama's right! Jus' maybe she sho is! Maybe I done gone foolish! Jus' maybe I has!"

He laughed so hard standing there, I thought he was going to cry. But then after a few moments he started walking again and the boys and I got right into step. Still chuckling, Mr Tom Bee said he couldn't rightly say he hadn't been called foolish before. In fact, he said, he'd been called foolish more times than he wanted to remember. Then he began to tell us about one of those times, and the boys and I listened eagerly. We loved to hear Mr Tom Bee tell his stories. With all his years, he had plenty of stories to tell too. He had seen the slavery days and he had seen the war that ended slavery. He had seen Confederate soldiers and he had seen Yankee soldiers. He had seen a lot of things over the years and he said he'd forgotten just about as much as he remembered. But as we walked the road listening to him I for one was mighty glad he had remembered as much as he had.

We reached Aunt Callie's, gave her the head medicine and the fish, then headed back towards home. Mr Tom Bee was still with us. He lived over our way. To get home we had to pass the Wallace store again. When we reached the crossroads, Mr Tom Bee said, "Y'all wait on up jus' another minute here. Done forgot my tobaccie." A truck and a wagon were now in front of the store. Mr Tom Bee took note of them and stepped onto the porch.

Jeremy Simms was still sitting on the porch, but he didn't say anything to us this time. He nodded slightly, that was all. I noticed he wasn't sucking on his candy cane; I could see it sticking out of his pocket. He bit his lip and looked around uneasily. We didn't say anything to him either. We just stood there wanting to get on home. It was getting late.

Mr Tom Bee entered the store. "'Ey there, John!" he called. "Give me some-a that chewin' tobaccie! Forgot to get it I was in before."

The boys and I, standing by the gas pump, looked

into the store. So did Jeremy. His father, Mr Charlie Simms, was in there now, sitting at the table by the stove along with his older teenage brothers, R.W. and Melvin. Dewberry and Thurston Wallace were there also and two white men we didn't know. They all turned their eyes on Mr Tom Bee. Dewberry and Thurston glanced at their father, and then Mr Charlie Simms spoke up. "Old nigger," he said, "who you think you talkin' to?"

Mr Tom Bee wet his lips. "Jus' . . . jus' come for my tobaccie."

Mr John Wallace glanced at the men, then, his jaw hardening, set eyes on Mr Tom Bee. "You bes' get on outa here, Tom."

Mr Tom Bee looked around at the men. His back straightened with that old, sharp-edged stubbornness. "Well, I sho do that, John," he said, "soon's I get me my tobaccie."

Mr Simms jumped up from the table. "John Wallace! You jus' gonna let this here old nigger talk t' ya this-a way? You gon' let him do that?"

Suddenly Stacey bounded up the steps to the store entrance. "We—we waitin' on ya, Mr Tom Bee!" he cried shrilly. "We waitin'! Come on, Mr Tom Bee! Come on!"

Mr Tom Bee looked over at him. He took a moment, then he nodded and I thought he was going to come on out. But instead he said, "Be right wit' ya, boy . . . soon's I get me my tobaccie." Then he turned again and faced John Wallace. "You—you gonna give me that tobaccie, John?"

Dewberry pulled from the counter. "Daddy! You don't shut this old nigger up, I'm gonna do it for ya!"

Mr John Wallace turned a mean look on his son and the look was enough to silence him. Then he looked around the room at Mr Simms, at R.W. and Melvin, at Thurston, at the two other white men gathered there. The store and all around it was plunged into silence.

Mr Tom Bee glanced nervously at the men, but he didn't stop. He seemed bent on carrying this thing through. "Well?" he asked of John Wallace. "I'm gonna get me that tobaccie?"

Silently John Wallace reached back to a shelf and got the tobacco. He placed it on the counter.

Mr Simms exploded. "What kind-a white man are ya, John Wallace, ya don't shut his black mouth? What kind-a white man?"

Mr Tom Bee looked at Mr Simms and the others, then went and picked up the tobacco. "Thank ya, John," he said. "Jus' put it on my charges there, John. Jus' put it on my charges." He glanced again at the men and started out. He got as far as the steps. The boys and I turned to go. Then we heard the click. The explosion of a shotgun followed and Mr Tom Bee tumbled down the steps, his right leg ripped open by the blast.

The boys and I stood stunned, just staring at Mr Tom Bee at first, not knowing what to do. Stacey started towards him, but Mr Tom Bee waved him back. "Get 'way from me, boy! Get 'way! Stacey, get them younguns back, 'way from me!" Stacey looked into the store, at the shotgun, and herded us across the road.

The white men came out and sniggered. Mr John Wallace, carrying the shotgun, came out onto the porch too. He stood there, his face solemn, and said, "You made me do that, Tom. I coulda killed ya, but I ain't wantin' to kill ya cause ya done saved my life an' I'm a Christian man so I ain't forgetting that. But this here disrespectin' me gotta stop and I means to stop it now. You gotta keep in mind you ain't nothin' but a nigger. You gonna learn to watch yo' mouth. You gonna learn to address me proper. You hear me, Tom?"

Mr Tom Bee sat in silence staring at the bloody leg.

"Tom, ya hear me?"

Now, slowly, Mr Tom Bee raised his head and looked up at John Wallace. "Oh, yeah, I hears ya all right. I hears ya. But let me tell you somethin', John. Ya was John t' me when I saved your sorry life and you give me your word you was always gonna be John t' me long as I lived. So's ya might's well go 'head and kill me cause that's what ya gon' be, John. Ya hear me, John? Till the Judgement Day. Till the earth opens itself up and the fires-a hell come takes yo' ungrateful soul! Ya hear me, John? Ya hear me? *John! John! John!* Till the Judgement Day! *John!*"

With that he raised himself to one elbow and began to drag himself down the road. The boys and I, candy canes in hand, stood motionless. We watched Mr John Wallace to see if he would raise the shotgun again. Jeremy, the candy cane in his pocket, watched too. We all waited for the second click of the shotgun. But only the cries of Mr Tom Bee as he inched his way along the road ripped the silence. *"John! John! John!"* he cried over and over again. "Ya hear me, John? Till the Judgement Day! John! *John! JOHN!"*

There was no other sound.

The Gold Cadillac

To Mother-Dear,
who has always been there for all of us
with her love and strength and understanding

The Gold Cadillac

My sister and I were playing out on the front lawn when the gold Cadillac rolled up and my father stepped from behind the wheel. We ran to him, our eyes filled with wonder. "Daddy, whose Cadillac?" I asked.

And Wilma demanded, "Where's our Mercury?"

My father grinned. "Go get your mother and I'll tell you all about it."

"Is it ours?" I cried. "Daddy, is it ours?"

"Get your mother!" he laughed. "And tell her to hurry!"

Wilma and I ran off to obey as Mr Pondexter next door came from his house to see what this new Cadillac was all about. We threw open the front door, ran through the downstairs front parlour and straight through the house to the kitchen where my mother was cooking and one of my aunts was helping her. "Come on, Mother-

Dear!" we cried together. "Daddy say come on out and see this new car!"

"What?" said my mother, her face showing her surprise. "What're you talking about?"

"A Cadillac!" I cried.

"He said hurry up!" relayed Wilma.

And then we took off again, up the back stairs to the second floor of the duplex. Running down the hall, we banged on all the apartment doors. My uncles and their wives stepped to the doors. It was good it was a Saturday morning. Everybody was home.

"We got us a Cadillac! We got us a Cadillac!" Wilma and I proclaimed in unison. We had decided that the Cadillac had to be ours if our father was driving it and holding on to the keys. "Come on see!" Then we raced on, through the upstairs sunroom, down the front steps, through the downstairs sunroom, and out to the Cadillac. Mr Pondexter was still there. Mr LeRoy and Mr Courtland from down the street were there too and all were admiring the Cadillac as my father stood proudly by, pointing out the various features.

"Brand-new 1950 Coup deVille!" I heard one of the men saying.

"Just off the showroom floor!" my father said. "I just couldn't resist it."

My sister and I eased up to the car and peeked in. It was all gold inside. Gold leather seats. Gold carpeting. Gold dashboard. It was like no car we had owned before. It looked like a car for rich folks.

"Daddy, are we rich?" I asked. My father laughed.

"Daddy, it's ours, isn't it?" asked Wilma, who was older and more practical than I. She didn't intend to give her heart too quickly to something that wasn't hers.

"You like it?"

"Oh, Daddy, yes!"

He looked at me. "What 'bout you, 'lois?"

"Yes, sir!"

My father laughed again. "Then I expect I can't much disappoint my girls, can I? It's ours all right!"

Wilma and I hugged our father with our joy. My uncles came from the house and my aunts, carrying their babies, came out too. Everybody surrounded the car and owwed and ahhed. Nobody could believe it.

Then my mother came out.

Everybody stood back grinning as she approached the car. There was no smile on her face. We all waited for her to speak. She stared at the car, then looked at my father, standing there as proud as he could be. Finally she said, "You didn't buy this car, did you, Wilbert?"

"Gotta admit I did. Couldn't resist it."

"But . . . but what about our Mercury? It was perfectly good!"

"Don't you like the Cadillac, Dee?"

"That Mercury wasn't even a year old!"

My father nodded. "And I'm sure whoever buys it is going to get themselves a good car. But we've got ourselves a better one. Now stop frowning, honey, and let's take ourselves a ride in our brand-new Cadillac!"

My mother shook her head. "I've got food on the

stove," she said and turning away walked back to the house.

There was an awkward silence and then my father said, "You know Dee never did much like surprises. Guess this here Cadillac was a bit too much for her. I best go smooth things out with her."

Everybody watched as he went after my mother. But when he came back, he was alone.

"Well, what she say?" asked one of my uncles.

My father shrugged and smiled. "Told me I bought this Cadillac alone, I could just ride in it alone."

Another uncle laughed. "Uh-oh! Guess she told you!"

"Oh, she'll come around," said one of my aunts. "Any woman would be proud to ride in this car."

"That's what I'm banking on," said my father as he went around to the street side of the car and opened the door. "All right! Who's for a ride?"

"We are!" Wilma and I cried.

All three of my uncles and one of my aunts, still holding her baby, and Mr Pondexter climbed in with us and we took off for the first ride in the gold Cadillac. It was a glorious ride and we drove all through the city of Toledo. We rode past the church and past the school. We rode through Ottawa Hills where the rich folks lived and on into Walbridge Park and past the zoo, then along the Maumee River. But none of us had had enough of the car so my father put the car on the road and we drove all the way to Detroit. We had plenty of family there and everybody was just as pleased as could be about the Cadillac. My father told our Detroit relatives that he was in the doghouse with my mother about buying the Cadillac. My uncles told them she wouldn't ride in the car. All the Detroit family thought that was funny and everybody, including my father, laughed about it and said my mother would come around.

It was early evening by the time we got back home, and I could see from my mother's face she had not come around. She was angry now not only about the car, but that we had been gone so long. I didn't understand that, since my father had called her as soon as we reached Detroit to let her know where we were. I had heard him myself. I didn't understand either why she did not like that fine Cadillac and thought she was being terribly disagreeable with my father. That night as she tucked Wilma and me in bed I told her that too.

"Is this your business?" she asked.

"Well, I just think you ought to be nice to Daddy. I think you ought to ride in that car with him! It'd sure make him happy."

"I think you ought to go to sleep," she said and turned out the light.

Later I heard her arguing with my father. "We're supposed to be saving for a house!" she said.

"We've already got a house!" said my father.

"But you said you wanted a house in a better neighbourhood. I thought that's what we both said!"

"I haven't changed my mind."

"Well, you have a mighty funny way of saving for it, then. Your brothers are saving for houses of their own and you don't see them out buying new cars every year!"

"We'll still get the house, Dee. That's a promise!"

"Not with new Cadillacs we won't!" said my mother and then she said a very loud good night and all was quiet.

The next day was Sunday and everybody figured that my mother would be sure to give in and ride in the Cadillac. After all, the family always went to church together on Sunday. But she didn't give in. What was worse she wouldn't let Wilma and me ride in the Cadillac either. She took us each by the hand, walked past the Cadillac where my father stood waiting and headed on towards the church, three blocks away. I was really mad at her now. I had been looking forward to driving up to the church in that gold Cadillac and having everybody see.

On most Sunday afternoons during the summertime, my mother, my father, Wilma, and I would go for a ride. Sometimes we just rode around the city and visited friends and family. Sometimes we made short trips over to Chicago or Peoria or Detroit to see relatives there or to Cleveland where we had relatives too, but we could also see the Cleveland Indians play. Sometimes we joined our aunts and uncles and drove in a caravan out to the park or to the beach. At the park or the beach Wilma and I would run and play. My mother and my aunts would spread a picnic and my father and my uncles would shine their cars.

But on this Sunday afternoon my mother refused to

ride anywhere. She told Wilma and me that we could go. So we left her alone in the big, empty house, and the family cars, led by the gold Cadillac, headed for the park. For a while I played and had a good time, but then I stopped playing and went to sit with my father. Despite his laughter he seemed sad to me. I think he was missing my mother as much as I was.

That evening my father took my mother to dinner down at the corner café. They walked. Wilma and I stayed at the house chasing fireflies in the back yard. My aunts and uncles sat in the yard and on the porch, talking and laughing about the day and watching us. It was a soft summer's evening, the kind that came every day and was expected. The smell of charcoal and of barbecue drifting from up the block, the sound of laughter and music and talk drifting from yard to yard were all a part of it. Soon one of my uncles joined Wilma and me in our chase of fireflies and when my mother and father came home we were at it still. My mother and father watched us for a while, while everybody else watched them to see if my father would take out the Cadillac and if my mother would slide in beside him to take a ride. But it soon became evident that the dinner had not changed my mother's mind. She still refused to ride in the Cadillac. I just couldn't understand her objection to it.

Though my mother didn't like the Cadillac, everybody else in the neighbourhood certainly did. That meant quite a few folks too, since we lived on a very busy block. On one corner was a grocery store, a cleaner's, and a gas station. Across the street was a beauty shop and a fish market, and down the street was a bar, another grocery store, the Dixie Theatre, the café, and a drugstore. There were always people strolling to or from one of these places and because our house was right in the middle of the block just about everybody had to pass our house and the gold Cadillac. Sometimes people took in the Cadillac as they walked, their heads turning for a longer look as they passed. Then there were people who just outright stopped and took a good look before continuing on their way. I was proud to say that car belonged to my family. I felt mighty important as people called to me as I ran down the street. "'Ey, 'lois! How's that Cadillac, girl? Riding fine?" I told my mother how much everybody liked that car. She was not impressed and made no comment.

Since just about everybody on the block knew everybody else, most folks knew that my mother wouldn't ride in the Cadillac. Because of that, my father took a lot of good-natured kidding from the men. My mother got kidded too as the women said if she didn't ride in that car, maybe some other woman would. And everybody laughed about it and began to bet on who would give in first, my mother or my father. But then my father said he was going to drive the car south into Mississippi to visit my grandparents and everybody stopped laughing.

My uncles stopped.

So did my aunts.

Everybody.

THE GOLD CADILLAC

"Look here, Wilbert," said one of my uncles, "it's too dangerous. It's like putting a loaded gun to your head."

"I paid good money for that car," said my father. "That gives me a right to drive it where I please. Even down to Mississippi."

My uncles argued with him and tried to talk him out of driving the car south. So did my aunts and so did the neighbours, Mr LeRoy, Mr Courtland and Mr Pondexter. They said it was a dangerous thing, a mighty dangerous thing, for a black man to drive an expensive car into the rural South.

"Not much those folks hate more'n to see a northern Negro coming down there in a fine car," said Mr Pondexter. "They see those Ohio licence plates, they'll figure you coming down uppity, trying to lord your fine car over them!"

I listened, but I didn't understand. I didn't understand why they didn't want my father to drive that car south. It was his.

"Listen to Pondexter, Wilbert!" cried another uncle. "We might've fought a war to free people overseas, but we're not free here! Man, those white folks down south'll lynch you soon's look at you. You know that!"

Wilma and I looked at each other. Neither one of us knew what *lynch* meant, but the word sent a shiver through us. We held each other's hand.

My father was silent, then he said: "All my life I've had to be heedful of what white folks thought. Well, I'm tired of that. I worked hard for everything I got. Got it honest, too. Now I got that Cadillac because I liked it and because it meant something to me that somebody like me from Mississippi could go and buy it. It's my car, I paid for it, and I'm driving it south."

My mother, who had said nothing through all this, now stood. "Then the girls and I'll be going too," she said.

"No!" said my father.

My mother only looked at him and went off to the kitchen.

My father shook his head. It seemed he didn't want us to go. My uncles looked at each other, then at my father. "You set on doing this, we'll all go," they said. "That way we can watch out for each other." My father took a moment and nodded. Then my aunts got up and went off to their kitchens too.

All the next day my aunts and my mother cooked and the house was filled with delicious smells. They fried chicken and baked hams and cakes and sweet potato pies and mixed potato salad. They filled jugs with water and punch and coffee. Then they packed everything in huge picnic baskets along with bread and boiled eggs, oranges and apples, plates and napkins, spoons and forks and cups. They placed all that food on the back seats of the cars. It was like a grand, grand picnic we were going on, and Wilma and I were mighty excited. We could hardly wait to start.

My father, my mother, Wilma and I got into the Cadillac. My uncles, my aunts, my cousins got into the Ford, the Buick, and the Chevrolet, and we rolled off in our caravan headed south. Though my mother was finally riding in the Cadillac, she had no praise for it. In fact, she said nothing about it at all. She still seemed upset and since she still seemed to feel the same about the car, I wondered why she had insisted upon making this trip with my father.

We left the city of Toledo behind, drove through Bowling Green and down through the Ohio countryside of farms and small towns, through Dayton and Cincinnati, and across the Ohio River into Kentucky. On the other side of the river my father stopped the car and looked back at Wilma and me and said, "Now from here on, whenever we stop and there're white people around, I don't want either one of you to say a word. *Not one word!* Your mother and I'll do all the talking. That understood?"

"Yes, sir," Wilma and I both said, though we didn't truly understand why.

My father nodded, looked at my mother and started the car again. We rolled on, down Highway 25 and through the bluegrass hills of Kentucky. Soon we began to see signs. Signs that read: WHITE ONLY, COLOURED NOT ALLOWED. Hours later, we left the Bluegrass State and crossed into Tennessee. Now we saw even more of the signs saying: WHITE ONLY, COLOURED NOT ALLOWED. We saw the signs above water fountains and in restaurant windows. We saw them in ice-cream parlours and at hamburger stands. We saw them in front of hotels and motels, and on the restroom doors of filling stations. I didn't like the signs. I felt as if I were in a foreign land.

I couldn't understand why the signs were there and I asked my father what the signs meant. He said they meant we couldn't drink from the water fountains. He said they meant we couldn't stop to sleep in the motels. He said they meant we couldn't stop to eat in the restaurants. I looked at the grand picnic basket I had been enjoying so much. Now I understood why my mother had packed it. Suddenly the picnic did not seem so grand.

Finally we reached Memphis. We got there at a bad time. Traffic was heavy and we got separated from the rest of the family. We tried to find them but it was no use. We had to go on alone. We reached the Mississippi state line and soon after we heard a police siren. A police car came up behind us. My father slowed the Cadillac, then stopped. Two white policemen got out of their car. They eyeballed the Cadillac and told my father to get out.

"Whose car is this, boy?" they asked.

I saw anger in my father's eyes. "It's mine," he said.

"You're a liar," said one of the policemen. "You stole this car."

"Turn around, put your hands on top of that car and spread-eagle," said the other policeman.

My father did as he was told. They searched him and I didn't understand why. I didn't understand either why they had called my father a liar and didn't believe that the Cadillac was his. I wanted to ask but I remembered my father's warning not to say a word and I obeyed that warning.

The policemen told my father to get in the back of the police car. My father did. One policeman got back into the police car. The other policeman slid behind the wheel of our Cadillac. The police car started off. The Cadillac followed. Wilma and I looked at each other and at our mother. We didn't know what to think. We were scared.

The Cadillac followed the police car into a small town and stopped in front of the police station. The policeman stepped out of our Cadillac and took the keys. The other policeman took my father into the police station.

"Mother-Dear!" Wilma and I cried. "What're they going to do to our daddy? They going to hurt him?"

"He'll be all right," said my mother. "He'll be all right." But she didn't sound so sure of that. She seemed worried.

We waited. More than three hours we waited. Finally my father came out of the police station. We had lots of questions to ask him. He said the police had given him a ticket for speeding and locked him up. But then the judge had come. My father had paid the ticket and they had let him go.

He started the Cadillac and drove slowly out of the town, below the speed limit. The police car followed us. People standing on steps and sitting on porches and in front of stores stared at us as we passed. Finally we were out of the town. The police car still followed. Dusk was falling. The night grew black and finally the police car turned around and left us.

We drove and drove. But my father was tired now

and my grandparents' farm was still far away. My father said he had to get some sleep and since my mother didn't drive, he pulled into a grove of trees at the side of the road and stopped.

"I'll keep watch," said my mother.

"Wake me if you see anybody," said my father.

"Just rest," said my mother.

So my father slept. But that bothered me. I needed him awake. I was afraid of the dark and of the woods and of whatever lurked there. My father was the one who kept us safe, he and my uncles. But already the police had taken my father away from us once today and my uncles were lost.

"Go to sleep, baby," said my mother. "Go to sleep."

But I was afraid to sleep until my father woke. I had to help my mother keep watch. I figured I had to help protect us too, in case the police came back and tried to take my father away again. There was a long, sharp knife in the picnic basket and I took hold of it, clutching it tightly in my hand. Ready to strike, I sat there in the back of the car, eyes wide, searching the blackness outside the Cadillac. Wilma, for a while, searched the night too, then she fell asleep. I didn't want to sleep, but soon I found I couldn't help myself as an unwelcome drowsiness came over me. I had an uneasy sleep and when I woke it was dawn and my father was gently shaking me. I woke with a start and my hand went up, but the knife wasn't there. My mother had it.

My father took my hand. "Why were you holding the knife, 'lois?" he asked.

I looked at him and at my mother. "I—I was scared," I said.

My father was thoughtful. "No need to be scared now, sugar," he said. "Daddy's here and so is Mother-Dear." Then after a glance at my mother, he got out of the car, walked to the road, looked down it one way, then the other. When he came back and started the motor, he turned the Cadillac north, not south.

"What're you doing?" asked my mother.

"Heading back to Memphis," said my father. "Cousin Halton's there. We'll leave the Cadillac and get his car. Driving this car any farther south with you and the girls in the car, it's just not worth the risk."

And so that's what we did. Instead of driving through Mississippi in golden splendour, we travelled its streets and roads and highways in Cousin Halton's solid, yet not so splendid, four-year-old Chevy. When we reached my grandparents' farm, my uncles and aunts were already there. Everybody was glad to see us. They had been worried. They asked about the Cadillac. My father told them what had happened, and they nodded and said he had done the best thing.

We stayed one week in Mississippi. During that week I often saw my father, looking deep in thought, walk off alone across the family land. I saw my mother watching him. One day I ran after my father, took his hand, and walked the land with him. I asked him all the questions that were on my mind. I asked him why the policemen had treated him the way they had and why people didn't want us to eat in the restaurants or drink from the water fountains or sleep in the hotels. I told him I just didn't understand all that.

My father looked at me and said that it all was a difficult thing to understand and he didn't really understand it himself. He said it all had to do with the fact that black people had once been forced to be slaves. He said it had to do with our skins being coloured. He said it had to do with stupidity and ignorance. He said it had to do with the law, the law that said we could be treated like this here in the South. And for that matter, he added, any other place in these United States where folks thought the same as so many folks did here in the South. But he also said, "I'm hoping one day though we can drive that long road down here and there won't be any signs. I'm hoping one day the police won't stop us just because of the colour of our skins and we're riding in a gold Cadillac with northern plates."

When the week ended, we said a sad good-bye to my grandparents and all the Mississippi family and headed in a caravan back towards Memphis. In Memphis we returned Cousin Halton's car and got our Cadillac. Once we were home my father put the Cadillac in the garage and didn't drive it. I didn't hear my mother say any more about the Cadillac. I didn't hear my father speak of it either.

Some days passed and then on a bright Saturday afternoon while Wilma and I were playing in the back yard, I saw my father go into the garage. He opened the garage doors wide so the sunshine streamed in, and began to shine the Cadillac. I saw my mother at the kitchen window staring out across the yard at my father. For a long time, she stood there watching my father shine his car. Then she came out and crossed the yard to the garage and I heard her say, "Wilbert, you keep the car."

He looked at her as if he had not heard.

"You keep it," she repeated and turned and walked back to the house.

My father watched her until the back door had shut behind her. Then he went on shining the car and soon began to sing. About an hour later he got into the car and drove away. That evening when he came back he was walking. The Cadillac was nowhere in sight.

"Daddy, where's our new Cadillac?" I demanded to know. So did Wilma.

He smiled and put his hand on my head. "Sold it," he said as my mother came into the room.

"But how come?" I asked. "We poor now?"

"No, sugar. We've got more money towards our new house now and we're all together. I figure that makes us about the richest folks in the world." He smiled at my mother and she smiled too and came into his arms.

After that we drove around in an old 1930s Model A Ford my father had. He said he'd factory-ordered us another Mercury, this time with my mother's approval. Despite that, most folks on the block figured we had fallen on hard times after such a splashy showing of good times and some folks even laughed at us as the Ford rattled around the city. I must admit that at first I was pretty much embarrassed to be riding around in that old Ford after the splendour of the Cadillac. But my father said to hold my head high. We and the family knew the truth. As fine as the Cadillac had been, he said, it had pulled us apart for a while. Now, as ragged and noisy as that old Ford was, we all rode in it together and we were a family again. So I held my head high.

Still though, I often thought of that Cadillac. We had had the Cadillac only a little more than a month, but I wouldn't soon forget its splendour or how I'd felt riding around inside it. I wouldn't soon forget either the ride we had taken south in it. I wouldn't soon forget the signs, the policemen, or my fear. I would remember that ride and the gold Cadillac all my life.

Also by Mildred D. Taylor

ROLL OF THUNDER, HEAR MY CRY

The Mississippi of the 1930s was a hard place for a black child to grow up in, but still Cassie didn't understand why farming his own land meant so much to her father. During that year, though, when the night riders were carrying hatred and destruction among her people, she learned about the great differences that divided them, and when it was worth fighting for a principle even if it brought terrible hardships.

LET THE CIRCLE BE UNBROKEN

For Cassie Logan, 1935 in the American deep south is a bewildering time: the Depression is tightening its grip, rich and poor are in conflict and racial tension is increasing. As she grows away from the security of childhood, Cassie struggles to understand the turmoil around her and the reasons for the deep-rooted fears of her family and friends.